This is a boy whose head is filled with wonder.

On the way to school,

he wonders where the
birds are flying.

"You've got your head in the clouds," sighs the park keeper,
as the boy nearly steps on his freshly-mown grass.

Waiting for the school bus,

he wonders who makes the clouds.

"Wake up, daydreamer!" grumbles the bus driver,
as the boy bumps into another passenger.

On the school crossing,

he wonders if the lollipop lady's sign
tastes as orange
as it looks.

"Pay attention to the road!" snaps the lollipop lady.

When he gets to school,

he wonders what
the best playground
in the world might
be like.

"No daydreaming today!" warns his form teacher.

In his science lesson,

he wonders how
the stars shine.

"You can't be scatterbrained in a laboratory!"
barks the science teacher.

In his art class, the boy finds
a blank square of paper waiting.

At first, he can't think of anything at all to draw.
"Just use your imagination," his art teacher tells him.

So he does.

As soon as his daydreams are set free,

they take off across the page...

...and the boy flies with them. Over a park where no one keeps off the grass.

Then soaring up into the sky,
where the cloud-makers
putter out candyfloss dreams.

He dives into the land where everything tastes as good as it looks.

Then joins the parade, around the best playground in the world.

school

And finally, far above it all,
where the galaxy-makers gather,
he helps them buff and polish
each shining star.

"Time to stop!" says his art teacher.

"I'd like each of you to come up
and show me what you have done."

Trembling, the boy walks slowly
to the front of the classroom...

"How wonderful!" gasps his art teacher. "It's like a daydream."

" What an incredible imagination you have."

Which of course is true,
because this is a boy whose head
is filled with wonder.

Enough to share with everyone.

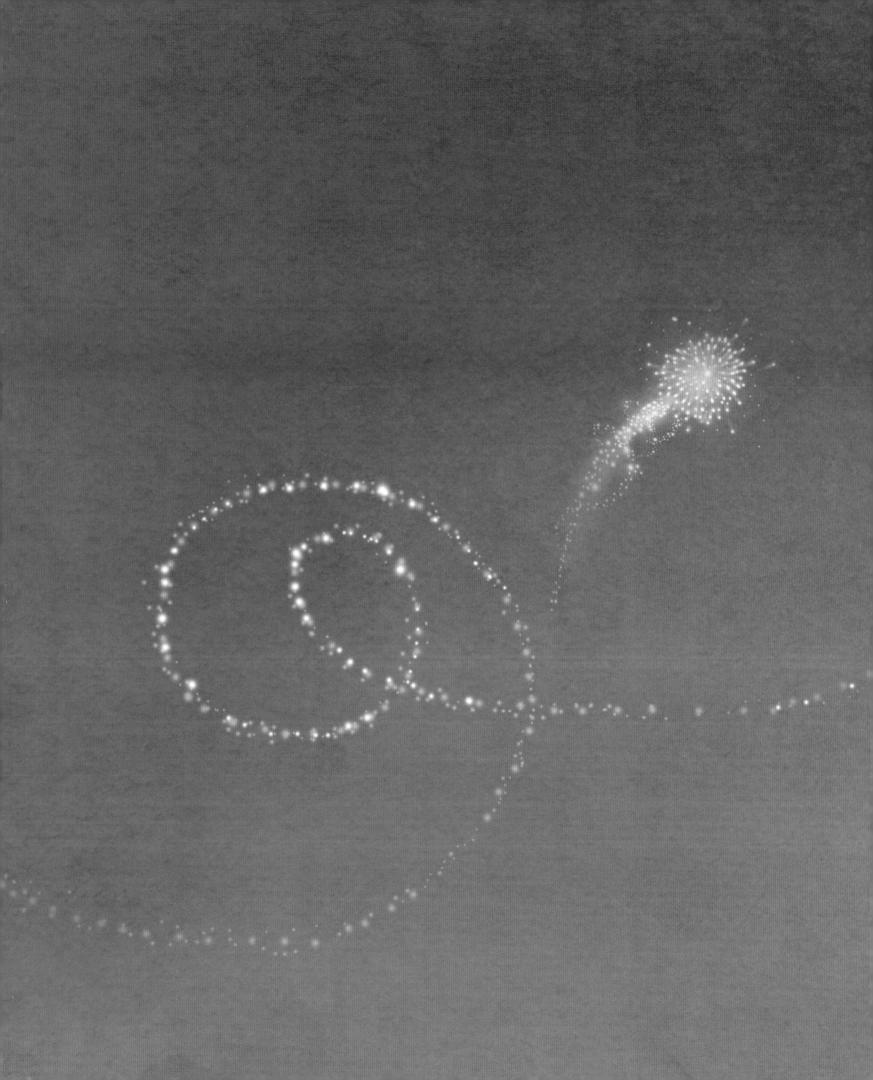

The

WONDER

by

Faye Hanson

A TEMPLAR BOOK

First published in the UK in 2014 by Templar Publishing,
an imprint of The Templar Company Limited,
Deepdene Lodge, Deepdene Avenue, Dorking, Surrey, RH5 4AT, UK
www.templarco.co.uk

ISBN 978-1-78370-074-5 (hardback)
ISBN 978-1-78370-114-8 (softback)

Edited by Libby Hamilton • Designed by Mike Jolley

Printed in China

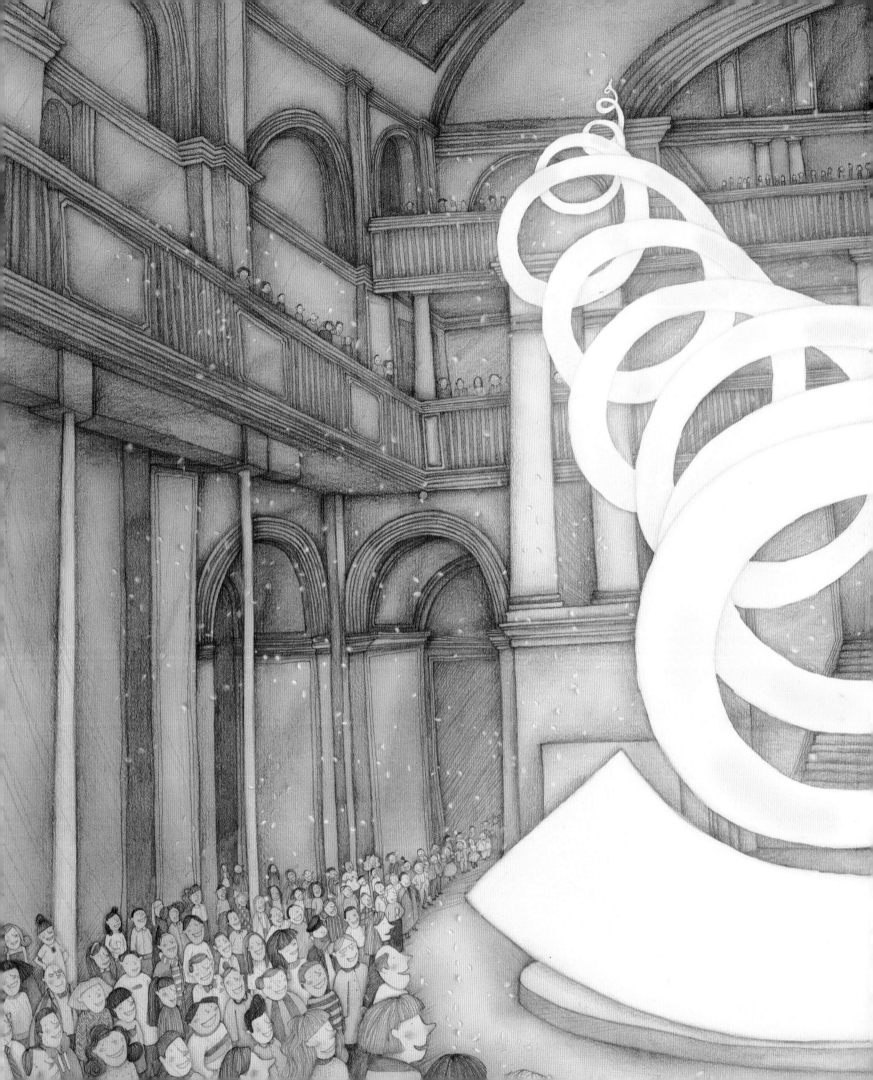